PLAY SOUL

10 soul classics for
CLARINET AND PIANO with CD

Arranged by Richard Harris

CLARINET PART

Contents

First published in 2007 by Faber Music Ltd
Music processed by Jackie Leigh
Cover design by Kenosha
Printed in England by Caligraving Ltd

ISBN10: 0-571-52461-3
EAN13: 978-0-571-52461-7

CD recorded in Wedgwood Studio, Surrey, October 2006
Backings created and engineered by Olly Wedgwood, ollywedgwood.com
Produced by Leigh Rumsey

BACKING TRACK 1

Respect

Words and Music by
Otis Redding

BACKING TRACK 2

I heard it through the grapevine

Words and Music by
Norman Whitfield and Barrett Strong

BACKING TRACK 3

Hello

Words and Music by
Lionel Richie

25
29
32
35
rit.
BACKING TRACK 4
I want you back
Words and Music by
Berry Gordy, Alphonso Mizell,
Frederick Perren and Deke Richards
Brightly ♩ = c.96
8
12
18
23
27
31
37

BACKING TRACK 5
Fallin'
Words and Music by
Alicia Augello-Cook
Dolce ed espressivo
mf freely
a tempo
(Moderate blues) ♩. = c.66
mp
mf
f
mp
f
4
mf
f
mp

PLAY SOUL

10 soul classics for
CLARINET AND PIANO with CD

Arranged by Richard Harris

Contents

First published in 2007 by Faber Music Ltd
Music processed by Jackie Leigh
Cover design by Kenosha
Printed in England by Caligraving Ltd

ISBN10: 0-571-52461-3
EAN13: 978-0-571-52461-7

CD recorded in Wedgwood Studio, Surrey, October 2006
Backings created and engineered by Olly Wedgwood, ollywedgwood.com
Produced by Leigh Rumsey

BACKING TRACK 1
Respect
Words and Music by
Otis Redding
Energetic ♩ = c.108
B♭7
E♭7
mf
F
E♭
f
opt. 8
(8)

17
F
E♭
F
E♭
opt. 8
21
B♭7
E♭7
B♭7
E♭7
(8)
25
f marcato
B♭7
E♭7
E♭/G
B♭
B♭7/D
E♭
f
(8)
29
B♭7
E♭7
B♭7
mf
(8)

BACKING TRACK 2

I heard it through the grapevine

Words and Music by
Norman Whitfield and Barrett Strong

19
G7
Dm
G/D Dm
G7
24
Dm
G/D Dm
ff
G7
ff
29
1.
mp
mf
Dm
p sotto voce
Dm7
mp
Em/D
33
2.
Dm
G/D
Dm
Em/D
Dm
G/D Dm
G/D
37
Dm7
Em/D Dm7
Em/D Dm
pp

BACKING TRACK 3

Hello

Words and Music by
Lionel Richie

18
Gm9 Gm9/F Ebmaj7 Gm/F Ebmaj7 Gm9 Gm9/F Ebmaj7 Gm/F Ebmaj7 Gm9 Gm9/F
mf dolce
mf
23
Ebmaj7 Gm/F Ebmaj7 Gm9 Gm9/F Ebmaj7 Gm/F Ebmaj7 Gm9 Gm9/F Ebmaj7 Gm/F Ebmaj7
f
28
Gm9 Gm9/F Ebmaj7 G Cm F Bb Eb
32
Ab D/F# Gm D7/A Gm/Bb D7/A Cm F Bb Eb
f
mf
36
rit.
Ab D Gm Gm/F Eb F Eb G
mp
mp

BACKING TRACK 4

I want you back

Words and Music by
Berry Gordy, Alphonso Mizell,
Frederick Perren and Deke Richards

14
B♭ Gm7 B♭/C Dm F/A B♭ F Gm7 B♭/C F Dm7
f
mf
18
B♭ Gm7 B♭/C Dm F/A B♭ F Gm7 B♭/C F N.C.
f
mp
22
F B♭
mf
26
Dm F/A B♭ F Gm7 B♭/C F
29
B♭ Dm F/A B♭ F Gm7 B♭/C F

33
Dm7
B♭
Gm7 B♭/C
Dm F/A B♭ F
Gm7 B♭/C F
37
Dm7
B♭
Gm7 B♭/C
Dm7 F/A B♭ F
Gm7 B♭/C F N.C.
BACKING TRACK 5
Fallin'
Words and Music by
Alicia Augello-Cook
Dolce ed espressivo
freely
a tempo
4
(Moderate blues) ♩. = c.66
Gm
Dm7
sim.

7
Gm
Dm7
mf
10
f
mf
13
16
mp
19

22
Gm
Dm7
Gm
D7
Gm
Dm7
25
Gm
Dm7
Gm
Dm7
Gm
D7
28
mf
f
Gm
Dm7sus4
Dm7
Gm
Dm7
Gm
Dm7
mp
mf
31
Gm
Dm7
Gm
Dm7
Gm
Dm7
mp

34
mp
Gm
Dm7
Gm
Dm7
Gm
p
BACKING TRACK 6
Baby love
Words and Music by
Brian Holland, Lamont Dozier and Eddie Holland
Brightly ♩= c.132
mf
Cm
A♭
F
B♭
mf
6
B♭/A♭
G
Cm
mp
11
B♭
Cm/E♭
B♭
Cm/E♭
B♭
f
mf

16
mf
E♭
B♭/D
Cm7
F7
B♭
B♭/A♭
G
mp
21
Cm
B♭
Cm/E♭
25
B♭
Cm/E♭
B♭
E♭
B♭/D
Cm7
F7
f
mf
30
mf
B♭
B♭/A♭
G
Cm
mp

34
B♭
E♭6
B♭
mf
38
E♭6
B♭
E♭
B♭/D
Cm7
F
B♭
mf
f
mf
43
B♭/A♭
G
Cm
B♭
f
f
48
Cm/E♭
B♭
Cm/E♭
B♭

BACKING TRACK 7

You're the first, the last, my everything

Words and Music by
Barry White, Tony Sepe and Peter Radcliffe

20
C7
F
Fmaj7
Dm
Dm7
mf
f
25
Fmaj9
F9
3
B♭maj7
B♭
3
30
B♭m
F
D7
3
1.
G7
C9
35
F
f
C
39
2.
C9
ff
F
ff

BACKING TRACK 8

Sittin' on the dock of the bay

Words and Music by
Otis Redding and Steve Cropper

F
C
B♭
E♭
A
G
D
Dm
repeat and fade

BACKING TRACK 9

Beat it

Words and Music by
Michael Jackson

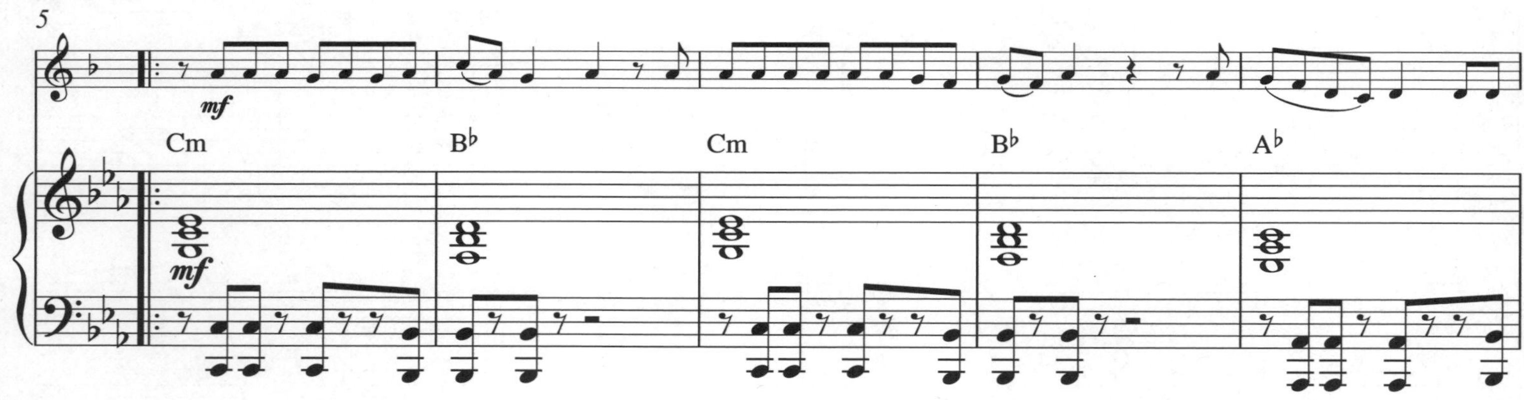

20
B♭
Cm
B♭
Cm
B♭6
f
24
Cm
B♭
Cm
B♭
28
1.
Cm
B♭
Cm
B♭
mf
33
2.
Cm
B♭
Cm
B♭
Cm
mf
mf

BACKING TRACK 10

I got you (I feel good)

Words and Music by
James Brown

17
B♭7
F7
mf
22
B♭7
C7
f
mf
mf
27
F7
f
3
31
B♭7
F7
3

35
1.
C7
B♭7
F9
f
39
2.
F9
f
C7
B♭7
43
F9
C7
B♭7
47
rit.
F9
ff
F7
ff

Baby love

BACKING TRACK 6

Words and Music by
Brian Holland, Lamont Dozier and Eddie Holland

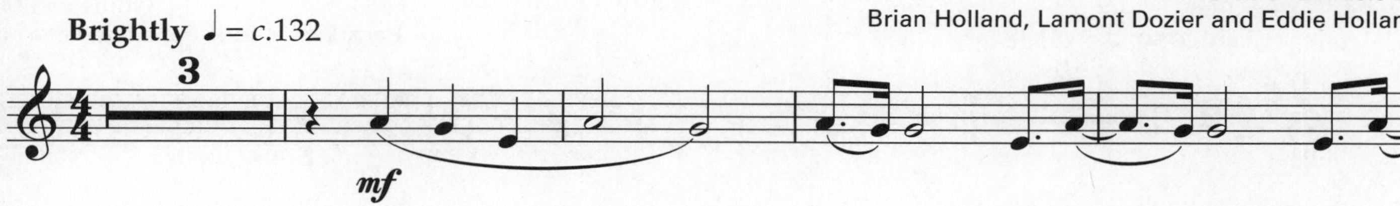

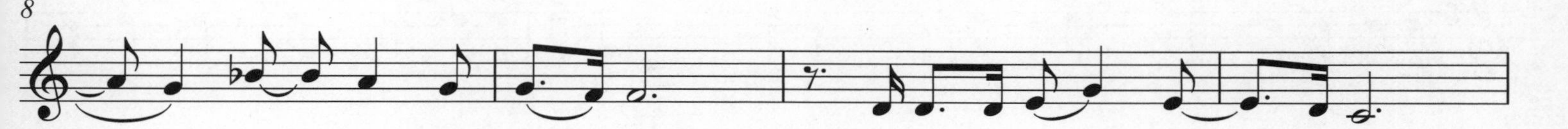

BACKING TRACK 7 You're the first, the last, my everything

Words and Music by
Barry White, Tony Sepe and Peter Radcliffe

BACKING TRACK 8 Sittin' on the dock of the bay

Words and Music by
Otis Redding and Steve Cropper

repeat and fade
BACKING TRACK 9
Beat it
Words and Music by
Michael Jackson
Vivace ♩ = c.144

BACKING TRACK 10

I got you (I feel good)

ISBN10: 0-571-52301-3
EAN13: 978-0-571-52301-6

- **Contains 10 standards, arrangements and original pieces with cool CD backing**
- **Includes 'Fly me to the moon', 'Stompin' at the Savoy' and 'C jam blues'**
- **Reflects a variety of jazz styles including swing, Latin, gospel and blues**
- **Has professional backing tracks for confident and atmospheric performance**
- **Includes a second, extended version of each piece for improvisation**
- **Ideal preparation for jazz exams, or simply for fun**
- **Carefully tailored for players of intermediate level (Grade 4–5)**